D1043481

DOVER
CHILDREN'S THRIFT CLASSICS

Beauty and the Beast
and Other Fairy Tales

MARIE LEPRINCE
DE BEAUMONT

AND

CHARLES PERRAULT

Illustrated by Kristine Bollinger

DOVER PUBLICATIONS, INC.
New York

DOVER CHILDREN'S THRIFT CLASSICS
EDITOR OF THIS VOLUME: THOMAS CROFTS

Copyright

Copyright © 1994 by Dover Publications, Inc.
Illustrations copyright © 1994 by Kristine Bollinger.

All rights reserved under Pan American and International Copyright Conventions.

Published in Canada by General Publishing Company, Ltd., 30 Lesmill Road, Don Mills, Toronto, Ontario.

Published in the United Kingdom by Constable and Company, Ltd., 3 The Lanchesters, 162–164 Fulham Palace Road, London W6 9ER.

Bibliographical Note

This Dover edition, first published in 1994, is a new selection of fairy tales by Mme. Marie Leprince de Beaumont and Charles Perrault, reprinted from *Old-Time Stories told by Master Charles Perrault* (which includes tales by other authors, including Leprince de Beaumont), translated by A. E. Johnson, as published by Dodd, Mead & Company, New York, in 1921. The translations of the verse morals are from *Perrault's Fairy Tales*, translated by S. R. Littlewood, as published by Herbert & Daniel, London, in 1912. An introductory Note and illustrations have been specially prepared for the present edition. For clarity, some difficult vocabulary has been simplified here and there.

Library of Congress Cataloging-in-Publication Data

Leprince de Beaumont, Madame (Jeanne-Marie), 1711–1780.
    Beauty and the beast and other fairy tales / Mme. Leprince de Beaumont and Charles Perrault ; illustrated by Kristine Bollinger.
        p.   cm.—(Dover children's thrift classics)
    "Translations from the French are from Old-time stories told by Master Charles Perrault . . . 1921. Translations of verse morals are from Perrault's fairy tales . . . 1912"—T.p. verso.
    Contents: Beauty and the beast — Blue Beard — Puss in Boots — The fairies — Little Tom Thumb — Ricky of the Tuft.
    ISBN 0-486-28032-2
    1. Fairy tales—France. [1. Fairy tales. 2. Folklore—France.] I. Perrault, Charles, 1628–1703. II. Bollinger, Kristine, ill. III. Title. IV. Series.
PZ8.L4784Be 1994
398.2'0944—dc20
                                                              94-14190
                                                              CIP
                                                              AC

Manufactured in the United States of America
Dover Publications, Inc., 31 East 2nd Street, Mineola, N.Y. 11501

Note

The six tales in this book come to us from two of the greatest authors of fairy stories, Mme. Marie Leprince de Beaumont (1711–1780) and Charles Perrault (1628–1703).

The first tale, "Beauty and the Beast," by Mme. Leprince de Beaumont, hardly needs an introduction. It is a classic of bravery, nobility and love. And, like every good fairy tale, it affords a glimpse into the dark side of human behavior.

The next five tales are all from Perrault, who was the first to record such standard plots of children's literature as "Cinderella," "Little Red Riding Hood" and "The Sleeping Beauty." This volume incorporates three of his other classics—"Little Tom Thumb," "Blue Beard" and "Puss in Boots"—along with two less well-known tales: "The Fairies," a tale of reward for goodness, and the witty "Ricky of the Tuft," which is similar in theme, if not in style, to "Beauty and the Beast."

Contents

List of Illustrations

Beauty and the Beast

O NCE UPON a time there lived a merchant who was exceedingly rich. He had six children—three boys and three girls—and being a sensible man he spared no expense upon their education, but engaged tutors of every kind for them. All his daughters were pretty, but the youngest especially was admired by everybody. When she was small she was known simply as "the little beauty," and this name stuck to her, causing a great deal of jealousy on the part of her sisters.

This youngest girl was not only prettier than her sisters, but very much nicer. The two elder girls were very arrogant as a result of their wealth; they pretended to be great ladies, declining to receive the daughters of other merchants, and associating only with people of quality. Every day they went off to balls and theatres, and for walks in the park, with many a gibe at their little sister, who spent much of her time in reading good books.

Now these girls were known to be very rich,

and in consequence were sought in marriage by many prominent merchants. The two eldest said they would never marry unless they could find a duke, or at least a count. But Beauty—this, as I have mentioned, was the name by which the youngest was known— very politely thanked all who proposed marriage to her, and said that she was too young at present, and that she wished to keep her father company for several years yet.

Suddenly the merchant lost his fortune, the sole property which remained to him being a small house in the country, a long way from the capital. With tears he broke it to his children that they would have to move to this house, where by working like peasants they might just be able to live.

The two elder girls replied that they did not wish to leave the town, and that they had several admirers who would be only too happy to marry them, notwithstanding their loss of fortune. But the simple maidens were mistaken: their admirers would no longer look at them, now that they were poor. Everybody disliked them on account of their arrogance, and folks declared that they did not deserve pity: in fact, that it was a good thing their pride had had a fall—a turn at minding sheep would teach them how to play the fine lady! "But we are very sorry for Beauty's misfortune," every-body added; "she is such a dear girl, and was always so considerate to poor people: so gen-tle, and with such charming manners!"

There were even several worthy men who would have married her, despite the fact that she was now penniless; but she told them she could not make up her mind to leave her poor father in his misfortune, and that she intended to go with him to the country, to comfort him and help him to work. Poor Beauty had been very grieved at first over the loss of her for-tune, but she said to herself:

"However much I cry, I shall not recover my wealth, so I must try to be happy without it."

When they were established in the country the merchant and his family started working on the land. Beauty used to rise at four o'clock in the morning, and was busy all day looking after the house, and preparing dinner for the family. At first she found it very hard, for she was not accustomed to work like a servant, but at the end of a couple of months she grew stronger, and her health was improved by the work. When she had leisure she read, or played the harpsichord, or sang at her spinning wheel.

Her two sisters, on the other hand, were bored to death; they did not get up till ten o'clock in the morning, and they idled about all day. Their only diversion was to bemoan the beautiful clothes they used to wear and the company they used to keep. "Look at our little sister," they would say to each other; "her tastes are so low and her mind so stupid that she is quite content with this miserable state of affairs."

The good merchant did not share the opinion of his two daughters, for he knew that Beauty was more fitted to shine in company than her sisters. He was greatly impressed by the girl's good qualities, and especially by her patience—for her sisters, not content with leaving her all the work of the house, never missed an opportunity of insulting her.

They had been living for a year in this seclusion when the merchant received a letter informing him that a ship on which he had some merchandise had just come safely home. The news nearly turned the heads of the two elder girls, for they thought that at last they would be able to quit their dull life in the country. When they saw their father ready to set out they begged him to bring them back dresses, furs, caps, and finery of every kind. Beauty asked for nothing, thinking to herself that all the money which the merchandise might yield would not be enough to satisfy her sisters' demands.

"You have not asked me for anything," said her father.

"As you are so kind as to think of me," she replied, "please bring me a rose, for there are none here."

Beauty had no real craving for a rose, but she was anxious not to seem to disparage the conduct of her sisters. The latter would have declared that she purposely asked for nothing in order to be different from them.

The merchant duly set forth; but when he reached his destination there was a lawsuit over his merchandise, and after much trouble he returned poorer than he had been before. With only thirty miles to go before reaching home, he was already looking forward to the pleasure of seeing his children again, when he found he had to pass through a large wood. Here he lost himself. It was snowing horribly; the wind was so strong that twice he was thrown from his horse, and when night came on he made up his mind he must either die of hunger and cold or be eaten by the wolves that he could hear howling all about him.

Suddenly he saw, at the end of a long avenue of trees, a strong light. It seemed to be some distance away, but he walked towards it, and presently discovered that it came from a large palace, which was all lit up.

The merchant thanked heaven for sending him this help, and hastened to the castle. To his surprise, however, he found no one about in the courtyards. His horse, which had followed him, saw a large stable open and went in; and on finding hay and oats in readiness the poor animal, which was dying of hunger, set to with a will. The merchant tied him up in the stable, and approached the house, where he found not a soul. He entered a large room; here there was a good fire, and a table laden with food, but with a place laid for one only. The rain and snow had soaked him to the skin, so he drew near the fire to dry himself. "I am sure," he remarked to himself, "that the master of this house or his servants will forgive the liberty I am taking; doubtless they will be here soon."

He waited some considerable time; but eleven o'clock struck and still he had seen nobody. Being no longer able to resist his hunger he took a chicken and devoured it in two mouthfuls, trembling. Then he drank several glasses of wine, and becoming bolder ventured out of the room. He went through several magnificently furnished apartments,

cannot prevent me from following you. Although I am young I am not so very deeply in love with life, and I would rather be devoured by this monster than die of the grief which your loss would cause me." Words were useless. Beauty was quite determined to go to this wonderful palace, and her sisters were not sorry, for they regarded her good qualities with deep jealousy.

The merchant was so taken up with the sorrow of losing his daughter that he forgot all about the box which he had filled with gold. To his astonishment, when he had shut the door of his room and was about to retire for the night, there it was at the side of his bed! He decided not to tell his children that he had become so rich, for his elder daughters would have wanted to go back to town, and he had resolved to die in the country. He did confide his secret to Beauty, however, and the latter told him that during his absence they had entertained some visitors, amongst whom were two admirers of her sisters. She begged her father to let them marry; for she was of such a sweet nature that she loved them, and forgave them with all her heart the evil they had done her.

When Beauty set off with her father the two heartless girls rubbed their eyes with an onion, so as to seem tearful; but her brothers wept in reality, as did also the merchant. Beauty alone did not cry, because she did not want to add to their sorrow.

The horse took the road to the palace, and by evening they espied it, all lit up as before. An empty stable awaited the nag, and when the good merchant and his daughter entered the great hall, they found there a table magnificently laid for two people. The merchant had not the heart to eat, but Beauty, forcing herself to appear calm, sat down and served him. Since the Beast had provided such splendid fare, she thought to herself, he must presumably be anxious to fatten her up before eating her.

When they had finished supper they heard a terrible noise. With tears the merchant bade farewell to his daughter, for he knew it was the Beast. Beauty herself could not help trembling at the awful apparition, but she did her best to compose herself. The Beast asked her if she had come of her own free will, and she timidly answered that such was the case.

"You are indeed kind," said the Beast, "and I am much obliged to you. You, my good man, will depart tomorrow morning, and you must not think of coming back again. Good-bye, Beauty!"

"Good-bye, Beast!" she answered.

Thereupon the monster suddenly disappeared.

"Daughter," said the merchant, embracing Beauty, "I am nearly dead with fright. Let me be the one to stay here!"

"No, father," said Beauty, firmly, "you must go tomorrow morning, and leave me to the mercy of Heaven. Perhaps pity will be taken on me."

They retired to rest, thinking they would not sleep at all during the night, but they were hardly in bed before their eyes were closed in sleep. In her dreams there appeared to Beauty a lady, who said to her:

"Your virtuous character pleases me, Beauty. In thus undertaking to give your life to save your father you have performed an act of goodness which shall not go unrewarded."

When she woke up Beauty related this dream to her father. He was somewhat consoled by it, but could not refrain from loudly giving vent to his grief when the time came to tear himself away from his beloved child.

As soon as he had gone Beauty sat down in the great hall and began to cry. But she had plenty of courage, and after imploring divine protection she determined to grieve no more during the short time she had yet to live.

She was convinced that the Beast would devour her that night, but made up her mind that in the interval she would walk about and have a look at this beautiful castle, the splendor of which she could not but admire.

Imagine her surprise when she came upon a door on which were the words "Beauty's Room"! She quickly opened this door, and was dazzled by the magnificence of the appointments within. "They are evidently anxious that I should not be bored," she murmured, as she caught sight of a large bookcase, a harpsichord, and several volumes of music. A moment later another thought crossed her mind. "If I had only a day to spend here," she reflected, "such provision would surely not have been made for me."

This notion gave her fresh courage. She opened the bookcase, and found a book in which was written, in letters of gold:

"Ask for anything you wish: you are mistress of all here."

"Alas!" she said with a sigh, "my only wish is to see my poor father, and to know what he is doing."

As she said this to herself she glanced at a large mirror. Imagine her astonishment when she perceived her home reflected in it, and saw her father just approaching. Sorrow was

written on his face; but when her sisters came
to meet him it was impossible not to detect,
despite the grimaces with which they tried to
simulate grief, the satisfaction they felt at the
loss of their sister. In a moment the vision
faded away, yet Beauty could not but think
that the Beast was very kind, and that she had
nothing much to fear from him.

At midday she found the table laid, and during her meal she enjoyed an excellent con-
cert, though the performers were invisible.
But in the evening, as she was about to sit
down at the table, she heard the noise made
by the Beast, and quaked in spite of herself.

"Beauty," said the monster to her, "may I
watch you have your supper?"

"You are master here," said the trembling
Beauty.

"Not so," replied the Beast; "it is you who
are mistress; you have only to tell me to go, if
my presence annoys you, and I will go immediately. Tell me, now, do you not consider me
very ugly?"

"I do," said Beauty, "since I must speak the
truth; but I think you are also very kind."

"It is as you say," said the monster; "and in
addition to being ugly, I lack intelligence. As I
am well aware, I am a mere beast."

"It is not the way with stupid people,"

answered Beauty, "to admit a lack of intelligence. Fools never realize it."

"Sup well, Beauty," said the monster, "and
try to banish dullness from your home—for
all about you is yours, and I should be sorry
to think you were not happy."

"You are indeed kind," said Beauty. "With
one thing, I must own, I am well pleased, and
that is your kind heart. When I think of that
you no longer seem to be ugly."

"Oh yes," answered the Beast, "I have a
good heart, right enough, but I am a monster."

"There are many men," said Beauty, "who
make worse monsters than you, and I prefer
you, notwithstanding your looks, to those
who under the semblance of men hide false,
corrupt, and ungrateful hearts."

The Beast replied that if only he had a grain
of wit he would compliment her in the grand
style by way of thanks; but that being so stupid he could only say he was much obliged.

Beauty ate with a good appetite, for she
now had scarcely any fear of the Beast. But
she nearly died of fright when he put this
question to her:

"Beauty, will you be my wife?"

For some time she did not answer, fearing
lest she might anger the monster by her
refusal. She summoned up courage at last to
say, rather fearfully, "No, Beast!"

She summoned up courage at last to say, rather
fearfully, "No, Beast!"

The poor monster gave forth so terrible a
sigh that the noise of it went whistling
through the whole palace. But to Beauty's
speedy relief the Beast sadly took his leave
and left the room, turning several times as he
did so to look once more at her. Left alone,
Beauty was moved by great compassion for
this poor Beast. "What a pity he is so ugly,"
she said, "for he is so good."

Beauty passed three months in the palace
quietly enough. Every evening the Beast paid
her a visit, and entertained her at supper by a
display of much good sense, if not with what
the world calls wit. And every day Beauty was
made aware of fresh kindnesses on the part of
the monster. Through seeing him often she
had become accustomed to his ugliness, and
far from dreading the moment of his visit, she
frequently looked at her watch to see if it was
nine o'clock, the hour when the Beast always
appeared.

One thing alone troubled Beauty; every
evening, before retiring to bed, the monster
asked her if she would be his wife, and
seemed overwhelmed with grief when she
refused. One day she said to him:

"You distress me, Beast. I wish I could
marry you, but I cannot deceive you by allow-
ing you to believe that that can ever be. I will
always be your friend—be content with that."

"Needs must," said the Beast. "But let me make the position plain. I know I am very terrible, but I love you very much, and I shall be very happy if you will only remain here. Promise that you will never leave me."

Beauty blushed at these words. She had seen in her mirror that her father was striken down by the sorrow of having lost her, and she wished very much to see him again. "I would willingly promise to remain with you always," she said to the Beast, "but I have so great a desire to see my father again that I shall die of grief if you refuse me this boon."

"I would rather die myself than cause you grief," said the monster. "I will send you back to your father. You shall stay with him, and your Beast shall die of sorrow at your departure."

"No, no," said Beauty, crying; "I like you too much to wish to cause your death. I promise you I will return in eight days. You have shown me that my sisters are married, and that my brothers have joined the army. My father is all alone; let me stay with him one week."

"You shall be with him tomorrow morning," said the Beast. "But remember your promise. All you have to do when you want to return is to put your ring on a table when you are going to bed. Good-bye, Beauty!"

As usual, the Beast sighed when he said these last words, and Beauty went to bed quite downhearted at having grieved him.

When she woke the next morning she found she was in her father's house. She rang a little bell which stood by the side of her bed, and it was answered by their servant, who gave a great cry at sight of her. The good man came running at the noise, and was overwhelmed with joy at the sight of his dear daughter. Their embraces lasted for more than a quarter of an hour. When their transports had subsided, it occurred to Beauty that she had no clothes to put on; but the servant told her that she had just discovered in the next room a chest full of dresses trimmed with gold and studded with diamonds. Beauty felt grateful to the Beast for this attention, and having selected the simplest of the gowns she bade the servant pack up the others, as she wished to send them as presents to her sisters. The words were hardly out of her mouth when the chest disappeared. Her father expressed the opinion that the Beast wished her to keep them all for herself, and in a trice dresses and chest were back again where they were before.

When Beauty had dressed she learned that her sisters, with their husbands, had arrived.

Both were very unhappy. The eldest had wedded an exceedingly handsome man, but the latter was so taken up with his own looks that he studied them from morning to night, and despised his wife's beauty. The second had married a man with plenty of brains, but he only used them to pay insults to everybody— his wife first and foremost.

The sisters were greatly mortified when they saw Beauty dressed like a princess, and more beautiful than the dawn. Her caresses were ignored, and the jealousy which they could not stifle only grew worse when she told them how happy she was. Out into the garden went the envious pair, there to vent their spleen to the full.

"Why should this brat be happier than we are?" each demanded of the other; "are we not much nicer than she is?"

"Sister," said the elder, "I have an idea. Let us try to persuade her to stay here longer than the eight days. Her stupid Beast will fly into a rage when he finds she has broken her word, and will very likely devour her."

"You are right, sister," said the other; "but we must make a great fuss over her if we are to make the plan successful."

With this plot decided upon they went upstairs again, and paid such attention to

their little sister that Beauty wept for joy.
When the eight days had passed the two sisters tore their hair, and showed such grief
over her departure that she promised to
remain another eight days.

Beauty reproached herself, nevertheless,
with the grief she was causing to the poor
Beast; moreover, she greatly missed not seeing him. On the tenth night of her stay in her
father's house she dreamed that she was in
the palace garden, where she saw the Beast
lying on the grass nearly dead, and that he
upbraided her for her ingratitude. Beauty
woke up with a start, and burst into tears.

"I am indeed very wicked," she said, "to
cause so much grief to a Beast who has
shown me nothing but kindness. Is it his fault
that he is so ugly, and has so few wits? He is
good, and that makes up for all the rest. Why
did I not wish to marry him? I should have
been a good deal happier with him than my
sisters are with their husbands. It is neither
good looks nor brains in a husband that make
a woman happy; it is beauty of character, virtue, kindness. All these qualities the Beast
has. I admit I have no love for him, but he has
my esteem, friendship, and gratitude. At all
events I must not make him miserable, or I
shall reproach myself all my life."

With these words Beauty rose and placed her ring on the table.

Hardly had she returned to her bed than she was asleep, and when she woke the next morning she saw with joy that she was in the Beast's palace. She dressed in her very best on purpose to please him, and nearly died of impatience all day, waiting for nine o'clock in the evening. But the clock struck in vain: no Beast appeared. Beauty now thought she must have caused his death, and rushed about the palace with loud despairing cries. She looked everywhere, and at last, recalling her dream, dashed into the garden by the canal, where she had seen him in her sleep. There she found the poor Beast lying unconscious, and thought he must be dead. She threw herself on his body, all her horror of his looks forgotten, and, feeling his heart still beat, fetched water from the canal and threw it on his face.

The Beast opened his eyes and said to Beauty:

"You forgot your promise. The grief I felt at having lost you made me resolve to die of hunger; but I die content since I have the pleasure of seeing you once more."

"Dear Beast, you shall not die," said Beauty; "you shall live and become my husband. Here and now I offer you my hand, and swear that I will marry none but you. Alas, I fancied I felt only friendship for you, but the sorrow I have experienced clearly proves to me that I cannot live without you."

Beauty had scarce uttered these words when the castle became ablaze with lights before her eyes: fireworks, music—all proclaimed a feast. But these splendors were lost on her: she turned to her dear Beast, still trembling for his danger.

Judge of her surprise now! At her feet she saw no longer the Beast, who had disappeared, but a prince, more beautiful than Love himself, who thanked her for having put an end to his enchantment. With good reason were her eyes riveted upon the prince, but she asked him nevertheless where the Beast had gone.

"You see him at your feet," answered the prince. "A wicked fairy condemned me to retain that form until some beautiful girl should consent to marry me, and she forbade me to betray any sign of intelligence. You alone in all the world could show yourself susceptible to the kindness of my character, and in offering you my crown I do but discharge the obligation that I owe you."

In agreeable surprise Beauty offered her hand to the handsome prince, and assisted

him to rise. Together they repaired to the castle, and Beauty was overcome with joy to find,
assembled in the hall, her father and her
entire family. The lady who had appeared to
her in her dream had had them transported to
the castle.

"Beauty," said this lady (who was a cele-
brated fairy), "come and receive the reward of
your noble choice. You preferred merit to
either beauty or wit, and you certainly
deserve to find these qualities combined in
one person. It is your destiny to become a
great queen, but I hope that the pomp of roy-
alty will not destroy your virtues. As for you,
ladies," she continued, turning to Beauty's
two sisters, "I know your hearts and the mal-
ice they harbor. Your doom is to become statues, and under the stone that wraps you
round to retain all your feelings. You will
stand at the door of your sister's palace, and I
can visit no greater punishment upon you
than that you shall be witnesses of her happiness. Only when you recognize your faults can
you return to your present shape, and I am
very much afraid that you will be statues for
ever. Pride, ill-temper, greed, and laziness can
all be corrected, but nothing short of a mira-
cle will turn a wicked and envious heart."

In a trice, with a tap of her hand, the fairy

transported them all to the prince's realm, where his subjects were delighted to see him again. He married Beauty, and they lived together for a long time in happiness the more perfect because it was founded on virtue.

Blue Beard

ONCE UPON a time there was a man who owned splendid town and country houses, gold and silver plate, tapestries and coaches gilt all over. But the poor fellow had a blue beard, and this made him so ugly and frightful that there was not a woman or girl who did not run away at sight of him.

Amongst his neighbors was a lady of high degree who had two surpassingly beautiful daughters. He asked for the hand of one of these in marriage, leaving it to their mother to choose which should be bestowed upon him. Both girls, however, raised objections, and his offer was bandied from one to the other, neither being able to bring herself to accept a man with a blue beard. Another reason for their distaste was the fact that he had already married several wives, and no one knew what had become of them.

In order that they might become better acquainted, Blue Beard invited the two girls, with their mother and three or four of their best friends, to meet a party of young men from the neighborhood at one of his country houses. Here they spent eight whole days, and throughout their stay there was a constant round of picnics, hunting and fishing expeditions, dances, dinners, and luncheons; and they never slept at all, through spending all the night in playing merry pranks upon each other. In short, everything went so gaily that the younger daughter began to think the master of the house had not so very blue a beard after all, and that he was an exceedingly agreeable man. As soon as the party returned to town their marriage took place.

At the end of a month Blue Beard informed his wife that important business obliged him to make a journey into a distant part of the country, which would occupy at least six weeks. He begged her to amuse herself well during his absence, and suggested that she should invite some of her friends and take them, if she liked, to the country. He was particularly anxious that she should enjoy herself thoroughly.

"Here," he said, "are the keys of the two large storerooms, and here is the one that locks up the gold and silver plate which is not in everyday use. This key belongs to the strongboxes where my gold and silver is kept, this to the caskets containing my jewels;

while here you have the master key which
gives admittance to all the apartments. As
regards this little key, it is the key of the small
room at the end of the long passage on the
lower floor. You may open everything, you
may go everywhere, but I forbid you to enter
this little room. And I forbid you so seriously
that if you were indeed to open the door, I
should be so angry that I might do anything."

She promised to follow out these instruc-
tions exactly, and after embracing her, Blue
Beard stepped into his coach and was off
upon his journey.

Her neighbors and friends did not wait to
be invited before coming to call upon the
young bride, so great was their eagerness to
see the splendors of her house. They had not
dared to venture while her husband was
there, for his blue beard frightened them. But
in less than no time there they were, running
in and out of the rooms, the closets, and the
wardrobes, each of which was finer than the
last. Presently they went upstairs to the storerooms, and there they could not admire
enough the profusion and magnificence of the
tapestries, beds, sofas, cabinets, tables, and
stands. There were mirrors in which they
could view themselves from top to toe, some
with frames of plate glass, others with frames

of silver and gilt lacquer, that were the most superb and beautiful things that had ever been seen. They were loud and persistent in their envy of their friend's good fortune. She, on the other hand, derived little amusement from the sight of all these riches, the reason being that she was impatient to go and inspect the little room on the lower floor.

So overcome with curiosity was she that, without reflecting upon the discourtesy of leaving her guests, she ran down a private staircase, so rapidly that twice or thrice she nearly broke her neck, and so reached the door of the little room. There she paused for a while, thinking of the prohibition which her husband had made, and reflecting that harm might come to her as a result of disobedience. But the temptation was so great that she could not conquer it. Taking the little key, with a trembling hand she opened the door of the room.

At first she saw nothing, for the windows were closed, but after a few moments she perceived dimly that the floor was entirely covered with clotted blood, and that in this were reflected the dead bodies of several women that hung along the walls. These were all the wives of Blue Beard, whose throats he had cut, one after another.

She thought to die of terror, and the key of the room, which she had just withdrawn from the lock, fell from her hand.

When she had somewhat regained her senses, she picked up the key, closed the door, and went up to her chamber to compose herself a little. But this she could not do, for her nerves were too shaken. Noticing that the key of the little room was stained with blood, she wiped it two or three times. But the blood did not go. She washed it well, and even rubbed it with sand and grit. Always the blood remained. For the key was bewitched, and there was no means of cleaning it completely. When the blood was removed from one side, it reappeared on the other.

Blue Beard returned from his journey that very evening. He had received some letters on the way, he said, from which he learned that the business upon which he had set forth had just been concluded to his satisfaction. His wife did everything she could to make it appear that she was delighted by his speedy return.

On the morrow he demanded the keys. She gave them to him, but with so trembling a hand that he guessed at once what had happened.

"How comes it," he said to her, "that the key

After several delays the key had to be brought.

of the little room is not with the others?"

"I must have left it upstairs upon my table," she said.

"Do not fail to bring it to me presently," said Blue Beard.

After several delays the key had to be brought. Blue Beard examined it, and addressed his wife.

"Why is there blood on this key?"

"I do not know at all," replied the poor woman, paler than death.

"You do not know at all?" exclaimed Blue Beard; "I know well enough. You wanted to enter the little room! Well, madam, enter it you shall—you shall go and take your place among the ladies you have seen there."

She threw herself at her husband's feet, asking his pardon with tears, and with all the signs of a true repentance for her disobedience. She would have softened a rock, in her beauty and distress, but Blue Beard had a heart harder than any stone.

"You must die, madam," he said; "and at once."

"Since I must die," she replied, gazing at him with eyes that were wet with tears, "give me a little time to say my prayers."

"I give you one quarter of an hour," replied

Blue Beard, "but not a moment longer."

When the poor girl was alone, she called her sister to her and said:

"Sister Anne"—for that was her name—"go up, I implore you, to the top of the tower, and see if my brothers are not approaching. They promised that they would come and visit me today. If you see them, make signs to them to hasten."

Sister Anne went up to the top of the tower, and the poor unhappy girl cried out to her from time to time:

"Anne, Sister Anne, do you see nothing coming?"

And Sister Anne replied:

"I see nought but dust in the sun and the green grass growing."

Presently Blue Beard, grasping a great cutlass, cried out at the top of his voice:

"Come down quickly, or I shall come upstairs myself."

"Oh please, one moment more," called out his wife.

And at the same moment she cried in a whisper:

"Anne, Sister Anne, do you see nothing coming?"

"I see nought but dust in the sun and the green grass growing."

"Come down at once, I say," shouted Blue Beard, "or I will come upstairs myself."

"I am coming," replied his wife.

Then she called:

"Anne, Sister Anne, do you see nothing coming?"

"I see," replied Sister Anne, "a great cloud of dust which comes this way."

"Is it my brothers?"

"Alas, sister, no; it is but a flock of sheep."

"Do you refuse to come down?" roared Blue Beard.

"One little moment more," exclaimed his wife.

Once more she cried:

"Anne, Sister Anne, do you see nothing coming?"

"I see," replied her sister, "two horsemen who come this way, but they are as yet a long way off. . . . Heaven be praised," she exclaimed a moment later, "they are my brothers. . . . I am signaling to them all I can to hasten."

Blue Beard let forth so mighty a shout that the whole house shook. The poor wife went down and cast herself at his feet, all disheveled and in tears.

"That avails you nothing," said Blue Beard; "you must die."

Seizing her by the hair with one hand, and

with the other brandishing the cutlass aloft, he made as if to cut off her head.

The poor woman, turning towards him and fixing a dying gaze upon him, begged for a brief moment in which to collect her thoughts.

"No! no!" he cried; "commend your soul to Heaven." And raising his arm——

At this very moment there came so loud a knocking at the gate that Blue Beard stopped short. The gate was opened, and two horsemen dashed in, who drew their swords and rode straight at Blue Beard. The latter recognized them as the brothers of his wife—one of them a dragoon, and the other a musketeer— and fled instantly in an effort to escape. But the two brothers were so close upon him that they caught him ere he could gain the first flight of steps. They plunged their swords through his body and left him dead. The poor woman was nearly as dead as her husband, and had not the strength to rise and embrace her brothers.

It was found that Blue Beard had no heirs, and so his wife became mistress of all his wealth. She devoted a portion to arranging a marriage between her sister Anne and a young gentleman with whom the latter had been for some time in love, while another portion purchased a captain's commission for each of her brothers. The rest formed a dowry for her own marriage with a very worthy man, who banished from her mind all memory of the evil days she had spent with Blue Beard.

Moral

Ladies, you should never pry,—
You'll repent it by and by!
'Tis the silliest of sins;
Trouble in a trice begins.
There are, surely—more's the woe!—
Lots of things you need not know.
Come, forswear it now and here—
Joy so brief, that costs so dear!

Another Moral

You can tell this tale is old
By the very way it's told.
Those were days of derring-do;
Man was lord, and master too.
Then the husband ruled as king.
Now it's quite a different thing;
Be his beard what hue it may—
Madam has a word to say!

Puss in Boots

A CERTAIN miller had three sons, and when he died the sole worldly goods which he bequeathed to them were his mill, his ass, and his cat. This little legacy was very quickly divided up, and you may be quite sure that neither notary nor attorney were called in to help, for they would speedily have grabbed it all for themselves.

The eldest son took the mill, and the second son took the ass. Consequently all that remained for the youngest son was the cat, and he was not a little disappointed at receiving such a miserable portion.

"My brothers," said he, "will be able to get a decent living by joining forces, but for my part, as soon as I have eaten my cat and made a muff out of his skin, I am bound to die of hunger."

These remarks were overheard by Puss, who pretended not to have been listening, and said very soberly and seriously:

"There is not the least need for you to worry, Master. All you have to do is to give me a pouch, and get a pair of boots made for me so that I can walk in the woods. You will find then that your share is not so bad after all."

Now this cat had often shown himself capable of performing cunning tricks. When catching rats and mice, for example, he would hide himself amongst the meal and hang downwards by the feet as though he were dead. His master, therefore, though he did not build too much on what the cat had said, felt some hope of being assisted in his miserable plight.

On receiving the boots which he had asked for, Puss gaily pulled them on. Then he hung the pouch round his neck, and holding the cords which tied it in front of him with his paws, he sallied forth to a warren where rabbits abounded. Placing some bran and lettuce in the pouch, he stretched himself out and lay as if dead. His plan was to wait until some young rabbit, unlearned in worldly wisdom, should come and rummage in the pouch for the eatables which he had placed there.

Hardly had he laid himself down when things fell out as he wished. A stupid young rabbit went into the pouch, and Master Puss, pulling the cords tight, killed him on the instant.

Well satisfied with his capture, Puss departed to the king's palace. There he demanded an audience, and was ushered upstairs. He entered the royal apartment, and bowed deeply to the king.

"I bring you, Sire," said he, "a rabbit from the warren of the marquis of Carabas" (such was the title he invented for his master), "which I am bidden to present to you on his behalf."

"Tell your master," replied the king, "that I thank him, and am pleased by his attention."

Another time the cat hid himself in a wheat field, keeping the mouth of his bag wide open. Two partridges ventured in, and by pulling the cords tight he captured both of them. Off he went and presented them to the king, just as he had done with the rabbit from the warren. His Majesty was not less gratified by the brace of partridges, and handed the cat a present for himself.

For two or three months Puss went on in this way, every now and again taking to the king, as a present from his master, some game which he had caught. There came a day when he learned that the king intended to take his daughter, who was the most beautiful princess in the world, for an excursion along the river bank.

"If you will do as I tell you," said Puss to his master, "your fortune is made. You have only to go and bathe in the river at the spot which I shall point out to you. Leave the rest to me."

The marquis of Carabas had no idea what plan was afoot, but did as the cat had directed.

While he was bathing the king drew near, and Puss at once began to cry out at the top of his voice:

"Help! help! the marquis of Carabas is drowning!"

At these shouts the king put his head out of the carriage window. He recognized the cat who had so often brought him game, and bade his escort go speedily to the help of the marquis of Carabas.

While they were pulling the poor marquis out of the river, Puss approached the carriage and explained to the king that while his master was bathing robbers had come and taken away his clothes, though he had cried "Stop, thief!" at the top of his voice. As a matter of fact, the rascal had hidden them under a big stone. The king at once commanded the keepers of his wardrobe to go and select a suit of his finest clothes for the marquis of Carabas.

The king received the marquis with many compliments, and as the fine clothes which the latter had just put on set off his good looks (for he was handsome and comely in appearance), the king's daughter found him very much to her liking. Indeed, the marquis of Carabas had not bestowed more than two or three respectful but sentimental glances upon her when she fell madly in love with him. The king invited him to enter the coach and join the party.

Delighted to see his plan so successfully launched, the cat went on ahead, and presently came upon some peasants who were mowing a field.

"Listen, my good fellows," said he, "if you do not tell the king that the field which you are mowing belongs to the marquis of Carabas, you will all be chopped up into little pieces like mincemeat."

In due course the king asked the mowers to whom the field on which they were at work belonged.

"It is the property of the marquis of Carabas," they all cried with one voice, for the threat from Puss had frightened them.

"You have inherited a fine estate," the king remarked to Carabas.

"As you see for yourself, Sire," replied the marquis; "this is a meadow which never fails to yield an abundant crop each year."

Still traveling ahead, the cat came upon some harvesters.

The ogre received him as civilly as an ogre can.

"Listen, my good fellows," said he, "if you do not declare that every one of these fields belongs to the marquis of Carabas, you will all be chopped up into little bits like mincemeat."

The king came by a moment later, and wished to know who was the owner of the fields in sight.

"It is the marquis of Carabas," cried the harvesters.

At this the king was more pleased than ever with the marquis.

Preceding the coach on its journey, the cat made the same threat to all whom he met, and the king grew astonished at the great wealth of the marquis of Carabas.

Finally Master Puss reached a splendid castle, which belonged to an ogre. He was the richest ogre that had ever been known, for all the lands through which the king had passed were part of the castle domain.

The cat had taken care to find out who this ogre was, and what powers he possessed. He now asked for an interview, declaring that he was unwilling to pass so close to the castle without having the honor of paying his respects to the owner.

The ogre received him as civilly as an ogre can, and bade him sit down.

"I have been told," said Puss, "that you have

the power to change yourself into any kind of animal—for example, that you can transform yourself into a lion or an elephant."

"That is perfectly true," said the ogre, curtly, "and just to prove it you shall see me turn into a lion."

Puss was so frightened on seeing a lion before him that he sprang onto the roof—not without difficulty and danger, for his boots were not meant for walking on the tiles.

Perceiving presently that the ogre had abandoned his transformation, Puss descended, and owned to having been thoroughly frightened.

"I have also been told," he added, "but I can scarcely believe it, that you have the further power to take the shape of the smallest animals—for example, that you can change yourself into a rat or a mouse. I confess that to me it seems quite impossible."

"Impossible?" cried the ogre; "you shall see!" And in the same moment he changed himself into a mouse, which began to run about the floor. No sooner did Puss see it than he pounced on it and ate it.

Presently the king came along, and noticing the ogre's beautiful mansion desired to visit it. The cat heard the rumble of the coach as it crossed the castle drawbridge, and running out to the courtyard cried to the king:

"Welcome, your Majesty, to the castle of the marquis of Carabas!"

"What's that?" cried the king. "Is this castle also yours, marquis? Nothing could be finer than this courtyard and the buildings which I see all about. With your permission we will go inside and look round."

The marquis gave his hand to the young princess, and followed the king as he led the way up the staircase. Entering a great hall they found there a magnificent lunch. This had been prepared by the ogre for some friends who were to pay him a visit that very day. The latter had not dared to enter when they learned that the king was there.

The king was now quite as charmed with the excellent qualities of the marquis of Carabas as his daughter. The latter was completely captivated by him. Noting the great wealth of which the marquis was evidently possessed, and having quaffed several cups of wine, he turned to his host, saying:

"It rests with you, marquis, whether you will be my son-in-law."

The marquis, bowing very low, accepted the honor which the king bestowed upon him. The very same day he married the princess.

Puss became a personage of great importance, and gave up hunting mice, except for amusement.

Moral

It's a pleasant thing, I'm told,
To be left a pile of gold.
But there's something better still,
Never yet bequeathed by will.
Leave a lad a stock of sense—
Though with neither pounds nor pence—
And he'll finish, as a rule,
Richer than the gilded fool.

Another Moral

Can the heart of a Princess
Yield so soon to borrowed dress?
So it seems—but wait a while—
'Tis not all a tale of guile.
He was young and straight of limb;
She was just the girl for him.
He was brave, and she was fair.
Tell me, when the right man's there—
Be he but a miller's son—
What Princess will not be won?

The Fairies

ONCE UPON a time there lived a widow with two daughters. The elder was often mistaken for her mother, so like her was she both in nature and in looks; parent and child being so disagreeable and arrogant that no one could live with them.

The younger girl, who took after her father in the gentleness and sweetness of her disposition, was also one of the prettiest girls imaginable. The mother doted on the elder daughter—naturally enough, since she resembled her so closely—and disliked the younger one as intensely. She made the latter live in the kitchen and work hard from morning till night.

One of the poor child's many duties was to go twice a day and draw water from a spring a good half-mile away, bringing it back in a large pitcher. One day when she was at the spring an old woman came up and begged for a drink.

"Why, certainly, good mother," the pretty lass replied. Rinsing her pitcher, she drew some water from the cleanest part of the spring and handed it to the dame, lifting up the jug so that she might drink the more easily.

Now this old woman was a fairy, who had taken the form of a poor village dame to see just how far the girl's good nature would go. "You are so pretty," she said, when she had finished drinking, "and so polite, that I am determined to bestow a gift upon you. This is the boon I grant you: with every word that you utter there shall fall from your mouth either a flower or a precious stone."

When the girl reached home she was scolded by her mother for being so long in coming back from the spring.

"I am sorry to have been so long, mother," said the poor child.

As she spoke these words there fell from her mouth three roses, three pearls, and three diamonds.

"What's this?" cried her mother; "did I see pearls and diamonds dropping out of your mouth? What does this mean, dear daughter?" (This was the first time she had ever addressed her daughter affectionately.)

The poor child told a simple tale of what had happened, and in speaking scattered diamonds right and left.

As she spoke there fell from her mouth three
roses, three pearls, and three diamonds.

"Really," said her mother, "I must send my own child there. Come here, Fanchon; look what comes out of your sister's mouth whenever she speaks! Wouldn't you like to be able to do the same? All you have to do is to go and draw some water at the spring, and when a poor woman asks you for a drink, give it her very nicely."

"Oh, indeed!" replied the ill-mannered girl; "don't you wish you may see me going there!"

"I tell you that you are to go," said her mother, "and to go this instant."

Very sulkily the girl went off, taking with her the best silver flagon in the house. No sooner had she reached the spring than she saw a lady, magnificently attired, who came towards her from the forest, and asked for a drink. This was the same fairy who had appeared to her sister, masquerading now as a princess in order to see how far this girl's ill-nature would carry her.

"Do you think I have come here just to get you a drink?" said the loutish damsel, arrogantly. "I suppose you think I brought a silver flagon here specially for that purpose—it's so likely, isn't it? Drink from the spring, if you want to!"

"You are not very polite," said the fairy, displaying no sign of anger. "Well, in return for your lack of courtesy I decree that for every word you utter a snake or a toad shall drop out of your mouth."

The moment her mother caught sight of her coming back she cried out, "Well, daughter?"

"Well, mother?" replied the rude girl. As she spoke a viper and a toad were spat out of her mouth.

"Gracious heavens!" cried her mother; "what do I see? Her sister is the cause of this, and I will make her pay for it!"

Off she ran to thrash the poor child, but the latter fled away and hid in the forest nearby. The king's son met her on his way home from hunting, and noticing how pretty she was inquired what she was doing all alone, and what she was weeping about.

"Alas, sir," she cried; "my mother has driven me from home!"

As she spoke the prince saw four or five pearls and as many diamonds fall from her mouth. He begged her to tell him how this came about, and she told him the whole story.

The king's son fell in love with her, and reflecting that such a gift as had been bestowed upon her was worth more than any dowry which another maiden might bring him, he took her to the palace of his royal father, and there married her.

As for the sister, she made herself so hateful that even her mother drove her out of the house. Nowhere could the wretched girl find anyone who would take her in, and at last she lay down in the forest and died.

Moral

Diamonds and rubies may
Work some wonders in their way;
But a gentle word is worth
More than all the gems on earth.

Another Moral

Though—when otherwise inclined—
It's a trouble to be kind,
Often it will bring you good
When you'd scarce believe it could.

Little Tom Thumb

ONCE UPON a time there lived a woodcutter and his wife, who had seven children, all boys. The eldest was only ten years old, and the youngest was seven. People were astonished that the woodcutter had had so many children in so short a time, but the reason was that his wife delighted in children, and never had less than two at a time.

They were very poor, and their seven children were a great tax on them, for none of them was yet able to earn his own living. And they were troubled also because the youngest was very delicate and could not speak a word. They mistook for stupidity what was in reality a mark of good sense.

This youngest boy was very little. At his birth he was scarcely bigger than a man's thumb, and he was called in consequence "Little Tom Thumb." The poor child was the scapegoat of the family, and got the blame for everything. All the same, he was the sharpest and shrewdest of the brothers, and if he spoke but little he listened much.

There came a very bad year, when the famine was so great that these poor people resolved to get rid of their family. One evening, after the children had gone to bed, the woodcutter was sitting in the chimney corner with his wife. His heart was heavy with sorrow as he said to her:

"It must be plain enough to you that we can no longer feed our children. I cannot see them die of hunger before my eyes, and I have made up my mind to take them tomorrow to the forest and lose them there. It will be easy enough to manage, for while they are amusing themselves by collecting sticks we have only to disappear without their seeing us."

"Ah!" cried the woodcutter's wife, "do you mean to say you are capable of letting your own children be lost?"

In vain did her husband remind her of their terrible poverty; she could not agree. She was poor, but she was their mother. In the end, however, reflecting what a grief it would be to see them die of hunger, she consented to the plan, and went weeping to bed.

Little Tom Thumb had heard all that was said. Having discovered, when in bed, that serious talk was going on, he had got up softly, and had slipped under his father's stool in order to listen without being seen. He went back to bed, but did not sleep a wink for the rest of the night, thinking over what he had better do. In the morning he rose very early and went to the edge of a brook. There he filled his pockets with little white pebbles and came quickly home again.

They all set out, and little Tom Thumb said not a word to his brothers of what he knew.

They went into a forest which was so dense that when only ten paces apart they could not see each other. The woodcutter set about his work, and the children began to collect twigs to make bundles. Presently the father and mother, seeing them busy at their task, edged gradually away, and then hurried off in haste along a little narrow footpath.

When the children found they were alone they began to cry and call out with all their might. Little Tom Thumb let them cry, being confident that they would get back home again. For on the way he had dropped the little white stones which he carried in his pocket all along the path.

"Don't be afraid, brothers," he said presently; "our parents have left us here, but I will take you home again. Just follow me."

They fell in behind him, and he led them straight to their house by the same path which they had taken to the forest. At first they dared not go in, but placed themselves against the door, where they could hear everything their father and mother were saying.

Now the woodcutter and his wife had no sooner reached home than the lord of the manor sent them a sum of ten crowns which had been owing from him for a long time, and of which they had given up hope. This put new life into them, for the poor creatures were dying of hunger.

The woodcutter sent his wife off to the butcher at once, and as it was such a long time since they had had anything to eat, she bought three times as much meat as a supper for two required.

When they found themselves once more at table, the woodcutter's wife began to lament.

"Alas! where are our poor children now?" she said; "they could make a good meal off what we have over. Mind you, William, it was you who wished to lose them: I declared over and over again that we should repent it. What are they doing now in that forest? Merciful heavens, perhaps the wolves have already eaten them! A monster you must be to lose your children in this way!"

At last the woodcutter lost patience, for she repeated more than twenty times that he would repent it, and that she had told him so.

He threatened to beat her if she did not hold her tongue.

It was not that the woodcutter was less grieved than his wife, but she browbeat him, and he was of the same opinion as many other people, who like a woman to have the knack of saying the right thing, but not the trick of being always in the right.

"Alas!" cried the woodcutter's wife, bursting into tears, "where are now my children, my poor children?"

She said it once so loud that the children at the door heard it plainly. Together they all cried out:

"Here we are! Here we are!"

She rushed to open the door for them, and exclaimed, as she embraced them:

"How glad I am to see you again, dear children! You must be very tired and very hungry. And you, Peterkin, how muddy you are — come and let me wash you!"

This Peterkin was her eldest son. She loved him more than all the others because he was inclined to be redheaded, and she herself was rather red.

They sat down at the table and ate with an appetite which it did their parents good to see. They all talked at once, as they recounted the fears they had felt in the forest.

The good souls were delighted to have their children with them again, and the pleasure continued as long as the ten crowns lasted. But when the money was all spent they relapsed into their former sadness. They again resolved to lose the children, and to lead them much further away than they had done the first time, so as to do the job thoroughly. But though they were careful not to speak openly about it, their conversation did not escape little Tom Thumb, who made up his mind to get out of the situation as he had done on the former occasion.

But though he got up early to go and collect his little stones, he found the door of the house doubly locked, and he could not carry out his plan.

He could not think what to do until the woodcutter's wife gave them each a piece of bread for breakfast. Then it occurred to him to use the bread in place of the stones, by throwing crumbs along the path which they took, and he tucked it tight in his pocket.

Their parents led them into the thickest and darkest part of the forest, and as soon as they were there slipped away by a side path and left them. This did not much trouble little Tom Thumb, for he believed he could easily find the way back wherever he walked. But to his dismay he could not discover a single crumb. The birds had come along and eaten it all.

They were in sore trouble now, for with every step they strayed further, and became more and more entangled in the forest. Night came on and a terrific wind arose, which filled them with dreadful alarm. On every side they seemed to hear nothing but the howling of wolves which were coming to eat them up. They dared not speak or move.

In addition it began to rain so heavily that they were soaked to the skin. At every step they tripped and fell on the wet ground, getting up again covered with mud, not knowing what to do with their hands.

Little Tom Thumb climbed to the top of a tree, in an endeavor to see something. Looking all about him he espied, far away on the other side of the forest, a little light like that of a candle. He got down from the tree, and was terribly disappointed to find that when he was on the ground he could see nothing at all.

After they had walked some distance in the direction of the light, however, he caught a glimpse of it again as they were nearing the edge of the forest. At last they reached the house where the light was burning, but not without much anxiety, for every time they had to go down into a hollow they lost sight of it.

They knocked at the door, and a good dame opened to them. She asked them what they wanted.

Little Tom Thumb explained that they were poor children who had lost their way in the forest, and begged her, for pity's sake, to give them a night's lodging.

Noticing what bonny children they all were, the woman began to cry.

"Alas, my poor little dears!" she said; "you do not know the place you have come to! Have you not heard that this is the house of an ogre who eats little children?"

"Alas, madam!" answered little Tom Thumb, trembling like all the rest of his brothers, "what shall we do? One thing is very certain: if you do not take us in, the wolves of the forest will devour us this very night, and that being so we should prefer to be eaten by your husband. Perhaps he may take pity on us, if you will plead for us."

The ogre's wife, thinking she might be able to hide them from her husband till the next morning, allowed them to come in, and put them to warm near a huge fire, where a whole sheep was cooking on the spit for the ogre's supper.

Just as they were beginning to get warm

they heard two or three great bangs at the door. The ogre had returned. His wife hid them quickly under the bed and ran to open the door.

The first thing the ogre did was to ask whether supper was ready and the wine opened. Then without ado he sat down to table. Blood was still dripping from the sheep, but it seemed all the better to him for that. He sniffed to right and left, declaring that he could smell fresh flesh.

"Indeed!" said his wife. "It must be the calf which I have just dressed that you smell."

"*I smell fresh flesh*, I tell you," shouted the ogre, eying his wife askance; "and there is something going on here which I do not understand."

With these words he got up from the table and went straight to the bed.

"Aha!" said he; "so this is the way you deceive me, wicked woman that you are! I have a very great mind to eat you too! It's lucky for you that you are old and tough! I am expecting three ogre friends of mine to pay me a visit in the next few days, and here is a tasty dish which will just come in nicely for them!"

One after another he dragged the children out from under the bed.

The poor things threw themselves on their

"I smell fresh flesh, I tell you," shouted the ogre.

knees, imploring mercy; but they had to deal with the most cruel of all ogres. Far from pitying them, he was already devouring them with his eyes, and repeating to his wife that when cooked with a good sauce they would make most dainty morsels.

Off he went to get a large knife, which he sharpened, as he drew near the poor children, on a long stone in his left hand.

He had already seized one of them when his wife called out to him. "What do you want to do it now for?" she said; "will it not be time enough tomorrow?"

"Hold your tongue," replied the ogre; "they will be all the more tender."

"But you have such a lot of meat," rejoined his wife; "look, there are a calf, two sheep, and half a pig."

"You are right," said the ogre; "give them a good supper to fatten them up, and take them to bed."

The good woman was overjoyed and brought them a splendid supper; but the poor little wretches were so cowed with fright that they could not eat.

As for the ogre, he went back to his drinking, very pleased to have such good entertainment for his friends. He drank a dozen cups more than usual, and was obliged to go off to bed early, for the wine had gone somewhat to his head.

Now the ogre had seven daughters who as yet were only children. These little ogresses all had the most lovely complexions, for, like their father, they ate fresh meat. But they had little round gray eyes, crooked noses, and very large mouths, with long and exceedingly sharp teeth, set far apart. They were not so very wicked at present, but they showed great promise, for already they were in the habit of killing little children to suck their blood.

They had gone to bed early, and were all seven in a great bed, each with a crown of gold upon her head.

In the same room there was another bed, equally large. Into this the ogre's wife put the seven little boys, and then went to sleep herself beside her husband.

Little Tom Thumb was fearful lest the ogre should suddenly regret that he had not cut the throats of himself and his brothers the evening before. Having noticed that the ogre's daughters all had golden crowns upon their heads, he got up in the middle of the night and softly placed his own cap and those of his brothers on their heads. Before doing so, he carefully removed the crowns of gold, putting them on his own and his brothers' heads. In this way, if the ogre were to feel like slaughtering them that night he would mistake the girls for the boys, and vice versa.

Things fell out just as he had anticipated. The ogre, waking up at midnight, regretted that he had postponed till the morrow what he could have done overnight. Jumping briskly out of bed, he seized his knife, crying: "Now then, let's see how the little rascals are; we won't make the same mistake twice!"

He groped his way up to his daughters' room, and approached the bed in which were the seven little boys. All were sleeping, with the exception of little Tom Thumb, who was numb with fear when he felt the ogre's hand, as it touched the head of each brother in turn, reach his own.

"Upon my word," said the ogre, as he felt the golden crowns; "a nice job I was going to make of it! It is very evident that I drank a little too much last night!"

Forthwith he went to the bed where his daughters were, and here he felt the little boys' caps.

"Aha, here are the little scamps!" he cried; "now for a smart bit of work!"

With these words, and without a moment's hesitation, he cut the throats of his seven daughters, and well satisfied with his work went back to bed beside his wife.

No sooner did little Tom Thumb hear him

snoring than he woke up his brothers, bidding them dress quickly and follow him. They crept quietly down to the garden, and jumped from the wall. All through the night they ran in haste and terror, without the least idea of where they were going.

When the ogre woke up he said to his wife:

"Go upstairs and dress those little rascals who were here last night."

The ogre's wife was astonished at her husband's kindness, never doubting that he meant her to go and put on their clothes. She went upstairs, and was horrified to discover her seven daughters bathed in blood, with their throats cut.

She fell at once into a swoon, which is the way of most women in similar circumstances.

The ogre, thinking his wife was very long in carrying out his orders, went up to help her, and was no less astounded than his wife at the terrible spectacle which confronted him.

"What's this I have done?" he exclaimed. "I will be revenged on the wretches, and quickly, too!"

He threw a jugful of water over his wife's face, and having brought her round ordered her to fetch his seven-league boots, so that he might overtake the children.

He set off over the countryside, and strode

far and wide until he came to the road along which the poor children were traveling. They were not more than a few yards from their home when they saw the ogre striding from hilltop to hilltop, and stepping over rivers as though they were merely tiny streams.

Little Tom Thumb espied near at hand a cave in some rocks. In this he hid his brothers, and himself followed them in, while continuing to keep a watchful eye upon the movements of the ogre.

Now the ogre was feeling very tired after so much fruitless marching (for seven-league boots are very fatiguing to their wearer), and felt like taking a little rest. As it happened, he went and sat down on the very rock beneath which the little boys were hiding. Overcome with weariness, he had not sat there long before he fell asleep and began to snore so terribly that the poor children were as frightened as when he had held his great knife to their throats.

Little Tom Thumb was not so alarmed. He told his brothers to flee at once to their home while the ogre was still sleeping soundly, and not to worry about him. They took his advice and ran quickly home.

Little Tom Thumb now approached the ogre and gently pulled off his boots, which he at once donned himself. The boots were very heavy and very large, but being enchanted boots they had the faculty of growing larger or smaller according to the leg they had to suit. Consequently they always fitted as though they had been made for the wearer.

He went straight to the ogre's house, where he found the ogre's wife weeping over her murdered daughters.

"Your husband," said little Tom Thumb, "is in great danger, for he has been captured by a gang of thieves, and the latter have sworn to kill him if he does not hand over all his gold and silver. Just as they had the dagger at his throat, he caught sight of me and begged me to come to you and thus rescue him from his terrible plight. You are to give me everything of value which he possesses, without keeping back a thing, otherwise he will be slain without mercy. As the matter is urgent he wished me to wear his seven-league boots, to save time, and also to prove to you that I am no impostor."

The ogre's wife, in great alarm, gave him immediately all that she had, for although this was an ogre who devoured little children, he was by no means a bad husband.

Little Tom Thumb, laden with all the ogre's wealth, forthwith repaired to his father's house, where he was received with great joy.

Many people do not agree about this last adventure, and pretend that little Tom Thumb never committed this theft from the ogre, and only took the seven-league boots, about which he had no compunction, since they were only used by the ogre for catching little children. These folks assert that they are in a position to know, having been guests at the woodcutter's cottage. They further say that when little Tom Thumb had put on the ogre's boots, he went off to the Court, where he knew there was great anxiety concerning the result of a battle which was being fought by an army two hundred leagues away.

They say that he went to the king and undertook, if desired, to bring news of the army before the day was out; and that the king promised him a large sum of money if he could carry out his project.

Little Tom Thumb brought news that very night, and this first errand having brought him into notice, he made as much money as he wished. For not only did the king pay him handsomely to carry orders to the army, but many ladies at the court gave him anything he asked to get them news of their lovers, and this was his greatest source of income. He was occasionally entrusted by wives with letters to their husbands, but they paid him so badly, and this branch of the business brought him in so little, that he did not even bother to reckon what he made from it.

After acting as courier for some time, and amassing great wealth thereby, little Tom Thumb returned to his father's house, and was there greeted with the greatest joy imaginable. He made all his family comfortable, buying newly created positions for his father and brothers. In this way he set them all up, not forgetting at the same time to look well after himself.

Moral

Children are a pride to all
When they're handsome, straight, and tall.
But how many homes must own
Some odd mite who's seldom shown—
Just a little pale-faced chap,
No one thinks is worth a rap!
Parents, brothers, laugh him down
Keep him mute with sneer and frown.
Yet it's Little Thumbling may
Bring them fortune one fine day!

Ricky of the Tuft

ONCE UPON a time there was a queen who bore a son so ugly and misshapen that for some time it was doubtful if he would have human form at all. But a fairy who was present at his birth promised that he should have plenty of brains, and added that by virtue of the gift which she had just bestowed upon him he would be able to impart to the person whom he should love best the same degree of intelligence which he possessed himself.

This somewhat consoled the poor queen, who was greatly disappointed at having brought into the world such a hideous brat. And indeed, no sooner did the child begin to speak than his sayings proved to be full of shrewdness, while all that he did was somehow so clever that he charmed everyone.

I forgot to mention that when he was born he had a little tuft of hair upon his head. For this reason he was called Ricky of the Tuft, Ricky being his family name.

Some seven or eight years later the queen

73

of a neighboring kingdom gave birth to twin daughters. The first one to come into the world was more beautiful than the dawn, and the queen was so overjoyed that it was feared her great excitement might do her some harm. The same fairy who had assisted at the birth of Ricky of the Tuft was present, and in order to moderate the transports of the queen she declared that this little princess would have no sense at all, and would be as stupid as she was beautiful.

The queen was deeply mortified, and a moment or two later her chagrin became greater still, for the second daughter proved to be extremely ugly.

"Do not be distressed, Madam," said the fairy; "your daughter shall be recompensed in another way. She shall have so much good sense that her lack of beauty will scarcely be noticed."

"May Heaven grant it!" said the queen; "but is there no means by which the elder, who is so beautiful, can be endowed with some intelligence?"

"In the matter of brains I can do nothing for her, Madam," said the fairy, "but as regards beauty I can do a great deal. As there is nothing I would not do to please you, I will bestow upon her the power of making beautiful any person who shall greatly please her."

As the two princesses grew up their perfections increased, and everywhere the beauty of the elder and the wit of the younger were the subject of common talk.

It is equally true that their defects also increased as they became older. The younger grew uglier every minute, and the elder daily became more stupid. Either she answered nothing at all when spoken to, or replied with some idiotic remark. At the same time she was so awkward that she could not set four china vases on the mantelpiece without breaking one of them, nor drink a glass of water without spilling half of it over her clothes.

Now although the elder girl possessed the great advantage which beauty always confers upon youth, she was nevertheless outshone in almost all company by her younger sister. At first everyone gathered round the beauty to see and admire her, but very soon they were all attracted by the graceful and easy conversation of the clever one. In a very short time the elder girl would be left entirely alone, while everybody clustered round her sister.

The elder princess was not so stupid that she was not aware of this, and she would willingly have surrendered all her beauty for half her sister's cleverness. Sometimes she was ready to die of grief, for the queen, though a sensible woman, could not refrain from occasionally reproaching her with her stupidity.

The princess had retired one day to a wood to bemoan her misfortune, when she saw approaching her an ugly little man, of very disagreeable appearance, but clad in magnificent attire.

This was the young prince Ricky of the Tuft. He had fallen in love with her portrait, which was everywhere to be seen, and had left his father's kingdom in order to have the pleasure of seeing and talking to her.

Delighted to meet her thus alone, he approached with every mark of respect and politeness. But while he paid her the usual compliments he noticed that she was plunged in melancholy.

"I cannot understand, madam," he said, "how anyone with your beauty can be so sad as you appear. I can boast of having seen many fair ladies, and I declare that none of them could compare in beauty with you."

"It is very kind of you to say so, sir," answered the princess; and stopped there, at a loss what to say further.

"Beauty," said Ricky, "is of such great advantage that everything else can be disregarded; and I do not see that the possessor of it can have anything much to grieve about."

To this the princess replied:

"I would rather be as plain as you are and have some sense, than be as beautiful as I am and at the same time stupid."

"Nothing more clearly displays good sense, madam, than a belief that one is not possessed of it. It follows, therefore, that the more one has, the more one fears it to be wanting."

"I am not sure about that," said the princess; "but I know only too well that I am very stupid, and this is the reason of the misery which is nearly killing me."

"If that is all that troubles you, madam, I can easily put an end to your suffering."

"How will you manage that?" said the princess.

"I am able, madam," said Ricky of the Tuft, "to bestow as much good sense as it is possible to possess on the person whom I love the most. You are that person, and it therefore rests with you to decide whether you will acquire so much intelligence. The only condition is that you shall consent to marry me."

The princess was dumbfounded, and remained silent.

"I can see," pursued Ricky, "that this suggestion perplexes you, and I am not surprised. But I will give you a whole year to make up your mind to it."

The princess had so little sense, and at the same time desired it so ardently, that she persuaded herself the end of this year would never come. So she accepted the offer which had been made to her. No sooner had she given her word to Ricky that she would marry him within one year from that very day, than she felt a complete change come over her. She found herself able to say all that she wished with the greatest ease, and to say it in an elegant, finished, and natural manner. She at once engaged Ricky in a brilliant and lengthy conversation, holding her own so well that Ricky feared he had given her a larger share of sense than he had retained for himself.

On her return to the palace amazement reigned throughout the Court at such a sudden and extraordinary change. Whereas formerly they had been accustomed to hear her give vent to silly, pert remarks, they now heard her express herself sensibly and very wittily.

The entire Court was overjoyed. The only person not too pleased was the younger sister, for now that she had no longer the advantage over the elder in wit, she seemed nothing but a little fright in comparison.

The king himself often took her advice, and several times held his councils in her apartment.

The news of this change spread abroad, and the princes of the neighboring kingdoms made many attempts to captivate her. Almost all asked her in marriage. But she found none with enough sense, and so she listened to all without promising herself to any.

At last came one who was so powerful, so rich, so witty, and so handsome, that she could not help being somewhat attracted by him. Her father noticed this, and told her she could make her own choice of a husband: she had only to declare herself.

Now the more sense one has, the more difficult it is to make up one's mind in an affair of this kind. After thanking her father, therefore, she asked for a little time to think it over.

In order to ponder quietly what she had better do she went to walk in a wood—the very one, as it happened, where she encountered Ricky of the Tuft.

While she walked, deep in thought, she heard beneath her feet a thudding sound, as though many people were running busily to and fro. Listening more attentively she heard voices. "Bring me that boiler," said one; then another—"Put some wood on that fire!"

At that moment the ground opened, and she saw below what appeared to be a large kitchen full of cooks and scullions, and all the train of attendants which the preparation of a great banquet involves. A gang of some twenty or thirty spit-turners emerged and took up their positions round a very long table in a path in the wood. They all wore their cook's caps on one side, and with their basting implements in their hands they kept time together as they worked, to the lilt of a melodious song.

The princess was astonished by this spectacle, and asked for whom their work was being done.

"For Prince Ricky of the Tuft, madam," said the foreman of the gang; "his wedding is tomorrow."

At this the princess was more surprised than ever. In a flash she remembered that it was a year to the very day since she had promised to marry Prince Ricky of the Tuft, and was taken aback by the recollection. The reason she had forgotten was that when she made the promise she was still without sense, and with the acquisition of that intelligence which the prince had bestowed upon her, all

At that moment the ground opened, and she saw
below what appeared to be a large kitchen.

memory of her former stupidities had been
blotted out.

She had not gone another thirty paces when
Ricky of the Tuft appeared before her, gallant
and resplendent, like a prince upon his wedding day.

"As you see, madam," he said, "I keep my
word to the minute. I do not doubt that you
have come to keep yours, and by giving me
your hand to make me the happiest of men."

"I will be frank with you," replied the princess. "I have not yet made up my mind on the
point, and I am afraid I shall never be able to
take the decision you desire."

"You astonish me, madam," said Ricky of
the Tuft.

"I can well believe it," said the princess,
"and undoubtedly, if I had to deal with a
clown, or a man who lacked good sense, I
should feel myself very awkwardly situated.
'A princess must keep her word,' he would
say, 'and you must marry me because you
promised to!' But I am speaking to a man of
the world, of the greatest good sense, and I
am sure that he will listen to reason. As you
are aware, I could not make up my mind to
marry you even when I was entirely without
sense; how can you expect that today, pos-
sessing the intelligence you bestowed on me,
which makes me still more difficult to please

than formerly, I should take a decision which I could not take then? If you wished so much to marry me, you were very wrong to relieve me of my stupidity, and to let me see more clearly than I did."

"If a man who lacked good sense," replied Ricky of the Tuft, "would be justified, as you have just said, in reproaching you for breaking your word, why do you expect, madam, that I should act differently where the happiness of my whole life is at stake? Is it reasonable that people who have sense should be treated worse than those who have none? Would you maintain that for a moment—you, who so markedly have sense, and desired so ardently to have it? But, pardon me, let us get to the facts. With the exception of my ugliness, is there anything about me which displeases you? Are you dissatisfied with my breeding, my brains, my disposition, or my manners?"

"In no way," replied the princess; "I like exceedingly all that you have displayed of the qualities you mention."

"In that case," said Ricky of the Tuft, "happiness will be mine, for it lies in your power to make me the most attractive of men."

"How can that be done?" asked the princess.

"It will happen of itself," replied Ricky of

the Tuft, "if you love me well enough to wish that it be so. To remove your doubts, madam, let me tell you that the same fairy who on the day of my birth bestowed upon me the power of endowing with intelligence the woman of my choice, gave to you also the power of endowing with beauty the man whom you should love, and on whom you should wish to confer this favor."

"If that is so," said the princess, "I wish with all my heart that you may become the handsomest and most attractive prince in the world, and I give you without reserve the boon which it is mine to bestow."

No sooner had the princess uttered these words than Ricky of the Tuft appeared before her eyes as the handsomest, most graceful and attractive man that she had ever set eyes on.

Some people assert that this was not the work of fairy enchantment, but that love alone brought about the transformation. They say that the princess, as she mused upon her lover's constancy, upon his good sense, and his many admirable qualities of heart and head, grew blind to the deformity of his body and the ugliness of his face; that his humpback seemed no more than was natural in a man who could make the courtliest of bows, and that the dreadful limp which had formerly distressed her now betokened nothing more than a certain diffidence and charming deference of manner. They say further that she found his eyes shine all the brighter for their squint, and that this defect in them was to her but a sign of passionate love; while his great red nose she found nought but martial and heroic.

However that may be, the princess promised to marry him on the spot, provided only that he could obtain the consent of her royal father.

The king knew Ricky of the Tuft to be a prince both wise and witty, and on learning of his daughter's regard for him, he accepted him with pleasure as a son-in-law.

The wedding took place upon the morrow, just as Ricky of the Tuft had foreseen, and in accordance with the arrangements he had long ago put in train.

Moral

Here's a fairy tale for you,
Which is just as good as true.
What we love is always fair,
Clever, deft, and debonair.

Another Moral

Nature oft, with open arms,
Lavishes a thousand charms;
But it is not these that bring
True love's truest offering.
'Tis some quality that lies
All unseen to other eyes—
Something in the heart or mind
Love alone knows how to find.